C000172025

FERRIS WHEEL THREESOME

GAY PUBLIC SEX SERIES #4

NICO FOX

CONTENTS

CHAPTER 1

ON MY THIRD and final day in Sin City, I sat alone in my hotel room on the Strip, flipping through channels and drinking champagne, on the company credit card, of course.

I'd had fun, but most of it was work-related. The software company I work for threw a conference for the employees and clients to celebrate a year of record sales.

Despite being only 28 years old, I impressed everybody by winning the best software salesperson of the year award at our closing ceremonies held at the Caesars Palace hotel.

Don't get me wrong, I love my coworkers, but most of them are in their 50s or 60s, and our activities were low key. The most exciting thing we did was see a magic show.

Last night, I checked out some of the gay bars. Not much of a scene compared to New York City, and I didn't even get laid. Thinking I'd have more luck tonight on Grindr, I changed my display name to "Last night in Vegas."

After several dick pics and short conversations that went nowhere, I didn't have any real takers. I wanted someone to come to my hotel room, because I didn't have a car, but locals didn't want to come to the Strip.

Just as I gave up and started to drift off to sleep, I heard that recognizable ding telling me that it was a notification from Grindr from the profile "Public Sex".

What an intriguing name! Maybe he knew some local cruising spots in the city or was just a wild child.

Public Sex: *Like ur pics. What u looking 4?*
Last night in Vegas: *Someone to pound my ass back to Manhattan*
Public Sex: *I think can provide that service :)*

He sent me a face picture. He was hot, probably in his early 20s, chiseled face covered in a one-day's growth of beard. His baby blues pierced through the photo.

Public Sex: *Pics?*

I sent him some of my best ass pics. I'm not too bad, if I say so myself, but my ass, that's my golden ticket. He sent a few of his girth-y glory. A match made in heaven.

Last night in Vegas: *I can host at Caesar's Palace. Endless champagne.*
Public Sex: *Did u read my profile name? Hotel sex = boring. I'll show u Vegas*
Last night in Vegas: *Already been 2 gay bars*
Public Sex: *I can give u a better time than the bars can. Things tourists miss*

Now we're talking. With a profile name that provocative, and a cock that magnificent, I could only imagine the fun we were going to have. Just the thought of it was exciting.

My cock started to rise through the soft, hotel robe. I'd been wearing it all night because it made me feel like a million bucks.

I started to stroke my cock, but then stopped because I wanted to make sure I saved it all for Mr. Public Sex. Maybe we'd do it in the desert. Hopefully, I wouldn't get bitten in the ass by a scorpion.

Last night in Vegas: *I'm Noah. UR?*
Public Sex: *First name: Hunter. Last name: Public Sex. LOL*

He sent me more shirtless pics, but it was the dick pics that made my mouth water. I wanted to drool all over it.

Public Sex: *Wanna get high?*
Last night in Vegas: *No drugs tonight. Early flight in the morning*
Public Sex: *Not talking about drugs :)*
Last night in Vegas: *Huh?*

He sent me a picture of the famous High Roller Ferris wheel.

Public Sex: *Meet me there in 1/2 hr - close to ur hotel*
Last night in Vegas: *just another tourist trap*
Public Sex: *Not when u c it like this!*

Was he really suggesting fooling around on the Ferris wheel? Isn't that risky?

That was the kind of thing I'd fantasized about, but never had the courage to do. It took all the strength in me not to rub one out right there just thinking about it.

Last night in Vegas: *Won't we get arrested?*
Public Sex: *Trust me, I know a guy that works there. Bring a jacket.*
Last night in Vegas: *CUS*

CHAPTER 2

I THOUGHT it was kinda odd that he asked me to bring a jacket. It hit 100 degrees that afternoon. But when I left the hotel, I couldn't believe the temperature drop in just a few hours. And the wind was fierce.

I met him at the hotel bar. There was only him and the bartender. He was even more stunning than his profile pics.

He wore a tight designer t-shirt that showed off his abs and chest. His arms were bursting out of the sleeves.

He looked at me but didn't get up or say anything. He just patted the bar stool next to him and I sat down. That sort of confidence is such a fucking turn-on.

"Two shots of vodka, my good sir," Hunter said. "Me and cutie here need some liquid courage."

The bartender laughed. I was just excited that he thought I was cute.

"I don't know what I'm more scared of: being arrested, or my fear of heights," I said.

He laughed. "You'll be too busy to even notice." He put his hand on my knee and held it there.

The sexual electricity was overwhelming. He grabbed my hand and put it on his leg, not too far from his crotch.

"Here you go, gentlemen," said the silver fox bartender. He looked over the counter and saw my hand on Hunter's leg.

"Hope this drink gets you where you need to go tonight." The bartender gave a knowing wink.

Feeling that the bartender was also gay, I relaxed a little, even gave a fleeting laugh in return. Hunter moved my hand over his crotch, and I squeezed his girth as it got hard.

He unzipped and pulled it from under his underwear and let it flap right there on the stool. It was so exhilarating to see him act in flagrant violation of public indecency laws.

The bartender turned around with two more shots. "Thought you might want a second round, on the house," he looked down at Hunter's crotch, which Hunter tried to cover, but to no avail.

My heart went into overdrive. I thought we'd be arrested right there. We were on camera. There was no way to deny it.

I'd be in jail and miss my flight tomorrow and I didn't even know anybody in Las Vegas that could bail me out. My work would find out and I'd be fired.

He gave a playful stern look to Hunter. "You know the rules here, Hunter. No flashing your dick unless you show the bartender, too."

The older gentleman reached over and gave a tug on Hunter's hard cock. Hunter seemed to enjoy being used as a piece of meat.

"I'll let you put your mouth on it for another free shot." Hunter dropped his pants down to his knees while still sitting on the bar stool. If someone were to talk in, we'd be in big trouble.

The bartender pretended to be offended before laughing. "You put that thing away before you get me fired. But I'll get you that free shot and maybe I can take a raincheck."

The bartender looked at me. "Besides, looks like Noah is on the menu tonight. Enjoy the wheel."

Hunter stuffed his cock back in his pants. "There are a few rules to follow on the Ferris wheel, and I know how to circumvent them. But you have to follow my lead, so we don't get caught."

We headed down the promenade toward the wheel, passing a few loud drunks enjoying their stay in Vegas.

At the entrance of the Ferris wheel, there were long metal railings that looked like it could hold a large crowd during busy periods, but there was nobody there except behind the ticket booth.

"Hunter. Didn't think you'd show up!" The guy behind the counter with a name tag that said "Caleb" came around to give him a hug. Then he turned to look at me. "Is this the catch of the evening?" He was tall, athletic and had slicked back golden locks like David Beckham.

Hunter laughed. "This is Noah. He's a High Roller virgin."

7

"Have fun you two. And don't forget, I can see ev-er-y-thing!" Caleb said.

We walked toward the escalators that led to the loading dock. "Is that true, that he can watch?"

"Yup. It's their job to make sure that no shenanigans happen while people are up there. But they look the other way for their friends."

"Can't other people see?"

"Nah, too dark. Probably will be empty this time of night," Hunter reassured me.

I didn't have time to be nervous about being watched having sex. Soon, my nerves about being up so high took over, and I trembled. It was pretty cute when Hunter put his hand on the small of my back to comfort me.

When the bottom of the Ferris wheel came into view, I was even more nervous. Instead of small gondolas to sit in, they were flying pods bigger than my tiny Manhattan apartment.

And they weren't empty. A few had several people in them. I wondered how we'd fool around when there were others in the pod.

"Are you ready for your date, Hunter?" asked Caleb as he walked us to the wheel. He looked me up and down and said, "Yum, can't wait to watch you get fucked."

It was a turn-on that this stranger was about to see me get pounded while naked in the sky. "Ah-hem," Caleb said while putting his hand out. Hunter took out a $50 bill and handed it to him. "Your secret is safe with us."

He smiled sarcastically as he rested his hand on my shoulder.

On the other side of the wheel where I presumed you exit, was another guy, deep into his phone and looking bored.

He didn't even look up at us. He was a little bit older, with a pony tail and wearing a Nirvana t-shirt.

"What about him? He looks straight," I said. "Or at least not into illegal public sex." Caleb laughed. "That's Kevin.

Straight, but ever heard of gay-for-pay? He's look-the-other-way-for-pay?"

I felt a little nauseous at depending on this guy to keep us safe, but he laughed. "He won't snitch on us."

Then he looked me straight in the eyes. "But just remember," he said, "I'll be watching your every move."

Caleb cupped my crotch and squeezed lightly then looked at Hunter and said, "I'm jealous you get to have him first."

First? What did he mean by that?

The Ferris wheel moves in a continuous circle and never stops. You have to enter the doorway while it's still moving, but since it goes so slow, it's not a problem.

When I realized that we would have a pod to ourselves, I understood what the fifty bucks was for.

There were screens at the top near the ceiling showing how the Ferris wheel was built and a running commentary about its size and history. Kinda distracting, but even more distracting was the beautiful view.

I could see the Bellagio, the Luxor, the Stratosphere, and out into the desert as far as the eye could see. And even this late at night, people strolled up and down the main strip, although they looked like ants from the Ferris wheel.

There was a bench on one side and Hunter sat down. Just like in the bar, he patted the seat for me to sit next to him, which I did. Our knees touched, and we kissed, but only briefly.

I checked around at the other pods to see what they could see. It's possible to see inside the other pods, especially if yours is above the one you are looking in. But I don't think the other people were paying much attention to Hunter and me.

We weren't doing anything, yet, and the view of Las Vegas couldn't be beat.

Hunter stroked his hard-on over his jeans and my heart raced. I was so worried we'd get caught. Sure, the ride operators agreed to look the other way, but what about the other riders?

His frisky fingers unzipped his jeans. His eyebrows furrowed as he looked straight into my eyes.

"You're really gonna do this? Whip it out here for everyone to see?"

We took off our jackets and placed them on our laps. My hand slipped under to get at the goods. Soon, he unzipped my pants, and he was stroking me too.

I still couldn't believe I was doing this in public. I lifted his jacket just enough so I could see his huge pole spring from under his underwear.

Almost at the top, the documentary voiceover stopped, and a loud alarm went off. Red lights flashed and then an announcement, "You are in violation of public indecency laws. We have alerted the police."

My heart jumped, and I shook. I'd be arrested, for sure. There goes my career. It'll be on my record for the rest of my life.

Hunter and I quickly took our hands out from under each other's jackets and looked around. I did an especially bad job of looking nonchalant.

Then another announcement came through, this time in Caleb's voice. "Just dicking around with you two. Get at it, studs."

He laughed into the microphone so that a distorted buzz rung through our pod. Hunter laughed as if he were in on the joke.

I sighed in relief but wasn't quite ready to get back into the action just yet. Then the wheel squeaked and made a loud crack as it slowed to a stop.

Not only did I lose sexual concentration, but this was one of the most gorgeous views I'd ever seen. We were at the very top.

"I wonder why the wheel stopped," I said to Hunter.

"That's included in my fifty bucks. None of the other pods can see us up here," he reassured me before his voice turned seductive and forceful. "Now drop 'em."

My palms were sweaty from being so high and my heart raced from the rush. Under my jacket, I lowered my jeans and underwear a couple of inches.

"That won't do." He threw my jacket to the other side of the pod, exposing me to the cameras and the whole of Las

Vegas airspace. "Stand up." I did as he said because his demanding voice was such a turn-on.

He pulled off my shirt, and I took off the rest of my clothes, standing there naked and looking down on the Strip.

Fluorescent reds and blue lights blinked along the main boulevard. I wondered if pilots flying above toward the nearby airport could see me naked.

Hunter stripped too and all I could do was marvel at his massive prick. Passion pulsed through my entire body.

I got on my knees and took his purple knob in my mouth, slurping and sucking. It didn't occur to me right away that Caleb was on the ground watching this through the security cameras. I wondered if he was jerking off to it.

Before I could really get a rhythm going, Hunter pulled me to my feet and leaned me over the bench. He lubed up my ass and penetrated me, slowly at first because I was so tight and resistant. As he sped up, my cock bobbed up and down.

Because I was face down, I couldn't see the TV screens near the ceiling, but when I turned my head up to get a glimpse, I flinched. Instead of videos of Las Vegas, they showed a live stream of me being fucked.

Security cameras aimed directly at my ass from three angles. I wondered...I hoped...that the other pods could see my humiliation. I wanted to be "Live in Las Vegas," a show that people from all over the world paid good money to see.

He gave short, hard thrusts as his fingernails dug into my shoulders. I held on to the bench for dear life, feeling its smooth texture. His grunts became louder and his shaft quivered until I could feel the jizz shoot into me.

As he pulled out, a rope of cum drizzled to the floor. It didn't even occur to me that we'd make a mess, but Hunter, being the pro that he is, pulled out some wet wipes and cleaned the sticky residue and put it into a spare plastic bag he brought.

Good thing he was organized.

When I stood up, I realized we had almost gone full circle and I had to hurry to get dressed. I moved towards my clothes before Hunter snatched them up off the floor to hold them for ransom.

"Not yet." He had a devilish grin on his face.

"Dude, I'm completely naked and there will but other customers that can see me. We'll definitely be arrested."

"We were the last customers. They're closed now." He looked at my naked body. "And you're not finished yet."

Caleb waited for us as our pod went toward the platform. He was laughing and hooting. Kevin was too, although he didn't get up from his stool. He didn't seem that interested.

Caleb held up his cell phone to show the video of me being fucked. "Did you want to buy a souvenir picture, so you have memories of your time in Vegas?"

"Please tell me you will not share that." I said.

"I'll never forget that *ooh* face you made when he shot his load in your ass. Classic PornHub video material."

I almost hyperventilated when he suggested he would post it online. I would be humiliated. Caleb stood in front of the exits, blocking us from getting out. "I promise to keep this hush, hush, but only if I have my turn."

Caleb turned to Kevin, "Can you take over controls? Twenty bucks in it for you."

"You horny gays," Kevin said. "I wish I could find a woman that was as open as you guys are. I'd get laid all the time." He laughed. "You guys have your butt fun. I'm going to look at boobs on my phone." We all laughed.

I nodded yes, not out of fear of being arrested or the video being shared, but because I wanted both of them to take me in the sky.

Caleb hopped on the wheel right as it left the platform again, so I couldn't get off at that point even if I wanted to.

CHAPTER 3

CALEB RIPPED off his shirt since he was the only one with clothes on. While Hunter was bulging with muscles, Caleb had more of a tight swimmer's build, but was just as hot.

He worked Hunter's flaccid cock back into attention with his hand. I circled Caleb's nipple with my tongue while Hunter lathered up his cock again with lube.

Caleb put his strong hands on my head and guided me down to my knees. I slid his shorts down and was greeted by a mushroom helmet that was ripe for the picking.

I sat back to appreciate his eight-inch meat before taking it in my mouth. He stiffened fully in my throat. He fucked my face without abandon.

I played with Caleb's balls until his trembling was unbearable and I thought he would come right then. I rolled my lips over that head and licked around it.

Behind me, Hunter took me by the hips and lifted my back end. Without missing a beat on Caleb's cock, I spread my cheeks for Hunter.

He rimmed me, licking the remnants of his own come from earlier. He teased his cock around the opening of my hole and entered me slowly.

There wasn't any pain this time because he spread me open earlier, so sped up quickly. Then he entered me with a powerful thrust, pushing me further onto Caleb's cock and I gagged. Caleb must have loved it because he kept moaning in pleasure.

The sound of their slurping came from above me as they kissed each other. All I could see was Caleb's thick pubic hair and the base of his cock moving in and out of my mouth. They rocked back and forth in tandem.

"Your turn," Hunter said, before either of them came.

Hunter pulled out and before long, Caleb's huge cock was buried in my ass. He lunged into me more powerfully than Hunter did. His cock was a perfect fit for my ass.

Although I couldn't see behind me, I felt one cock go out and other one in. They shared me between them and after a while, I lost count of which dick was which. I didn't care. I just wanted them both to take control of my ass.

While they fucked me, I spit on my own cock and stared stroking. I thought I would explode. I begged them for more. More dick. More force. This was heaven.

One dick convulsed and shot inside of me. After a few seconds of heavy breathing, he withdrew, and I was instantly filled with another cock.

This one drove energetically into me before bursting through and filling me up. I never found out who came in me first.

As the overflow of come dripped out of my ass, I stroked myself until I shot my load on the bench and knew we'd have to do another clean-up job. I was completely exhausted and couldn't even get up.

Caleb joked, "Almost back to base. Wanna do round three?"

Hunter laughed. "I'm spent."

I'm glad Hunter spoke up, because my ass was sore as fuck. The three of us got dressed just as the wheel came back to the ground.

We got off and Kevin held out his hand. Caleb handed him a twenty. Kevin shrugged and drew his attention back to his phone. The exit of the Ferris wheel goes through a gift shop that was now closed.

Just outside the shop, it surprised me to see the bartender from earlier in the evening.

"Good job, kid. I'll always treasure the video." The bartender waved a flash drive in my face. "What happens in Vegas, stays on my hard drive." He chuckled.

My flight back to New York was in three hours. I took a cab back to the hotel, grabbed a shower and headed straight to the airport. I slept like a baby on the flight home.

ABOUT THE AUTHOR

Hi, I'm Nico. I love to write gay stories about public sex, cruising, bathhouses, anything taboo and a little bit dirty.

When I'm not writing, I love hanging out at the bars and binge-watching Netflix alike.

If you enjoyed this book, sign up for the Mailing List and receive a **FREE** book.

See you next time

-Nico

Join the Mailing List

For more information:
www.NicoFoxAuthor.com

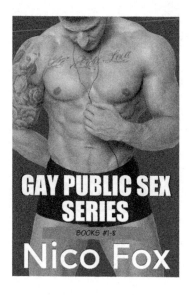

The complete Gay Public Sex Series box set. **Eight** steamy M/M erotic stories full of **public** encounters.

This bundle includes:

Bulge on a Train

Truck Stop Fantasy

Fitting Room Temptation

Ferris Wheel Threesome

Hole in the Wall Exhibitionist

Ride-Share Stripper

Gay Resort Weekend

Art Gallery Awakening

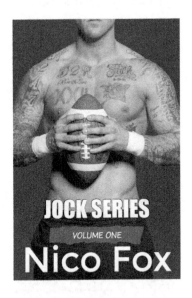

The first Jock Series box set. **Six** steamy M/M erotic stories full of **sweaty athletic guys**.

This bundle includes:

Captain of the Swim Team

First Time, First Down

Soccer Jockstrap

Slammed By the Team

Team Catcher

Heavyweight Punch

The first DILF Series box set. Six stories about **hot daddies** and their younger counterparts.

This bundle includes:

DILF of My Dreams

Seduced by the DILF

My Boss is a DILF

First Time Gay with My Girlfriend's Dad

My Girlfriend's Dad Wants It

First Time Gay with the DILF Professor

"I always follow his lead about anything and everything. All of our friends do. He uses his charm and imposing stature to convince us to do anything he wants."

Finn always had a crush on his best friend, Cameron, who is *very* popular with the girls. Standing next to well-built, captain of the football team, and all-around stud Cameron makes Finn feel a little, shall we say, less than...insecure.

Cameron has always protected Finn from others when they make fun of him for his small stature and he's always felt secure with him.

Finn invites Cameron over for a night of video games and beer only to be shocked when Cameron makes a wager on a game that Finn can't say no to. Who says fantasies don't come true?

Dustin has landed his dream job in Silicon Valley just one month after graduating college. He tries to keep his head down as much as he can, despite being surrounded by **hyper-masculine alphas** that call each other ***bro.*** He just can't stop lusting after the company's founder, notorious womanizer and billionaire's son, Brett.

The company is in peril. A bug in their software may cause one of their biggest customers to leave them. Everyone in the office is nervous, but they try to cover it up with heavy drinking after work and carrying on with their secret Santa ritual.

But Dustin solves the bug, making him the company hero. Brett is eternally grateful to his new employee for saving his company. Find out how this straight stud will pay back his employee in this new erotic story from Nico Fox.

A SEXY underground Halloween party...

"It's amazing how far two people in love will go to hide their inner desires from each other."

Lucas is a shy college student. His boyfriend, Colton, is an extroverted sports stud that every guy on campus wants to get with. Together, they have the perfect relationship. Or so it seems.

Lucas is worried someone will steal Colton away because he's such a catch. What's more, Lucas doesn't know if he can trust himself to handle monogamy.

They head into Manhattan to look for the perfect Halloween costumes for their upcoming school party. They want sexy costumes to show off all that hard work in the gym.

At the costume store, they meet Ace, a sophisticated New Yorker throwing his own Halloween party, one where inhibitions are thrown to the wind.

Ace seems a little shady. The party is so elusive that they need to be blindfolded as they ride in a limo to the party. But that's the price Lucas is willing to pay to go to a real New York City party.

How will Lucas and Colton's relationship hold up after a wild night at the party? Will jealousy get in the way, or will exploration bring their relationship to new heights?

Printed in Great Britain
by Amazon

23397237R00020